Shopping with O

by Donald W. Kruse   Illustrated by Aeryn Meyer

Shopping with Orville! by Donald W. Kruse, Illustrated by Aeryn Meyer,
is published by:

ZACCHEUS ENTERTAINMENT

Shopping with Orville! Copyright © 2020 by Donald W. Kruse

All rights reserved worldwide, including the right to reproduce this book or portions thereof in any form whatsoever. For comments or questions write to:

Zaccheus Entertainment
P.O. Box 23
Minong, WI 54859

ISBN: 978-0-9997854-0-9

1st Edition 2007
2nd Edition 2020

Manufactured in the United States of America

A special thank you from the author to Aeryn Meyer, Joyce DeWitt, and Arte Johnson.

Other Books by Donald W. Kruse

Jasper Has Left the Building!

Jasper and the Haunted House!

Jasper Has Returned!

Hey, Charlie!

Pee-Pee Harley and the Bandit!

Where's the Gold?

Dear Joey

Moose Pee and Tea!

That's Not a Pickle!
Parts 1 through 7

Gorilla Soup!

Blitz and Blatz!

Beebs Goes Camping!

Beebs Cooks a Turkey!

Beebs Goes Fishing!

Chicken Britches!

Monster at O'Malley's Mansion

Waldo, Blue, and Glad Max Too!

Take a Bath—Please!

What Do You Feed a Snow Snoot?

There's a Goof on My Roof!

Jasper Meets the Martians!

Cluck, Cluck, Cluck...SPLASH!

Fleas, Please!

Ragdolly's Love

Please Turn Green!

What's That Smell?

If I Ever Go To The Moon...

No Thanks, Simon!

Don't Have a Cow!

INTRODUCTION

I wish I had kids to read this story to but Minke, my dog, listened with rapt attention. She smiled and woofed, so ***Shopping with Orville!*** by Donald W. Kruse has my total endorsement.

—Arte Johnson

FOREWORD

Shopping with Orville! by Donald W. Kruse is a lovely tale that lets children know no matter what silliness we may have done in the past, we all have it in us to reach out and help one another—and that behavior brings love, respect, and appreciation.

—Joyce DeWitt

This is Orville,
wearing a small red hat.
Orville is *not* a mouse—
Orville is my pet rat.

And this is me and Orville,
sitting in a church pew.
We go every Sunday,
as most Christians do.

And afterwards,
we go home to play.
And when the day is done,
we always pray.

Orville likes swinging ...
and Orville likes singing.

Orville likes winning ...
and Orville likes swimming.

5

Orville likes riding and sliding
and even some hopping.
But most of all,
Orville loves shopping!

One day I grabbed Orville
by his little rat wrist.
"It's time to go shopping—
Mother gave me a list!"

We looked both ways
when crossing the street.
Then Orville and I
were craving a sweet.

7

So Orville and I went
to the candy store first.
He ate so much chocolate,
I thought he might burst!

He left candy wrappers
throughout the store.
And he spilled lots of candy
all over the floor!

Then he fell inside
a jar of licorice,
and the candy whips
made him ticklish.

I pulled him out
and straightened his hat,
then proceeded to scold
that naughty rat.

But with a single bound
he found the gumball machine,
and stuffed his mouth with gumballs.
They were red, white, and green!

"No more gumballs for you,
little Orville," I said.
Then I paid the clerk
whose face was now red.

Then we went to the hardware store
to buy electrical tape for Dad.
And a huge display of grass seed
made Orville exceptionally glad.

"Don't eat that, Orville!"
I said.
"You have to plant it and grow it,
then mow it, instead."

But Orville had made
yet another big mess.
And the man behind the counter
was mad, I guess.

For he had grass seed in his ears,
and grass seed in his hair.
He had grass seed in his pockets,
and some in his underwear!

I paid for the tape
and a half bag of seed,
which wasn't on the list—
something Dad didn't need.

"GET OUT! GET OUT!"
shouted the hardware store man.
And Orville clung to his hat,
as the two of us ran.

Next, we went to the store
that fills us with joy.
We went to the store
that sells lots of toys!

There were dolls, stuffed animals,
and model airplanes …
toy cars and trucks,
and even some trains!

Orville hopped aboard
and rode the caboose.
But the train derailed
and slammed into a goose.

Then Orville eyed the plane
and was airborne in a *flash*!
He buzzed the store
before hitting the fan,
and then that airplane *crashed*!

"Orville, are you okay?" I asked,
broken fan blades on his back.
Then he stood and tossed them aside,
knocking train cars off their track.

The store clerk approached—
a big, angry man—
and with pinwheel eyes,
he told us to **SCRAM!**

19

Next, we went to the store
where they sell ice cream.
But when the lady saw Orville,
she started to scream!

"SKUNK! SKUNK!"
I heard the lady yell.
"Get him out of my store
before the whole place smells!"

"This is *not* a skunk!" I said.
"Please don't get upset.
Orville is a *rat*,
and he's my favorite pet."

One Hundred and Thirty-one Flavors!

21

"GET OUT!" she shouted,
throwing ice cream and cones.
Then we caught one scoop …
then two scoops …
and we sat eating alone.

"Having a good time, Orville?"
I asked,
as he licked his cone clean.
He nodded his head, "yes,"
then begged more ice cream.

"No more for now, Orville," I said,
straightening his hat.
"We have more shopping to do
before we go back."

23

Next, we went to the store
where they sell all kinds of food.
Orville shot through the doors,
in a very good mood.

First, he ran to the aisle
where they store all the flour.
And he tried to be good
with all of his power.

But it was far too much
for Orville to resist.
He was sinking in flour,
so I grabbed his wrist.

Then Orville found the sugar
in a white paper sack.
He gnawed on a corner,
and he never looked back.

Soon all that was showing
was his long naked tail.
And women pushing carts
started to wail.

"EEEEEK!" they shrieked.
"IT'S A RAT! IT'S A RAT!"
Then the manager came running,
carrying a bat.

27

"Watch out for the bat, Orville!"
I yelled.
Then the manager swung …
and missed …
and then he fell.

I snatched my little Orville
and tried to get outside.
But the manager stopped us
and hissed, "I'll tan your hides!"

We were trapped in a corner,
with no way of escape.
"We have to be going now," I said.
"It's getting quite late."

But the manager held us
by the scruff of our necks.
"Just look what you did.
My store is a wreck!"

Then Orville flicked flour
right off of his tail,
dusting the manager's face—
now white as a sail.

As he wiped away flour,
and while blinking his eyes,
the manager said sternly,
"I've had it with you guys."

Just then the lights went out
in the big grocery store.
People yelled and hollered,
as they ran for the doors.

The manager shouted,
"THE POWER IS OUT!
SOMETHING IS BROKEN!
THE DOORS WILL NOT WORK.
THE DOORS WILL NOT OPEN!"

The people were trapped,
and in the dark they screamed.
Then the manager got a flashlight
and turned on its beam.

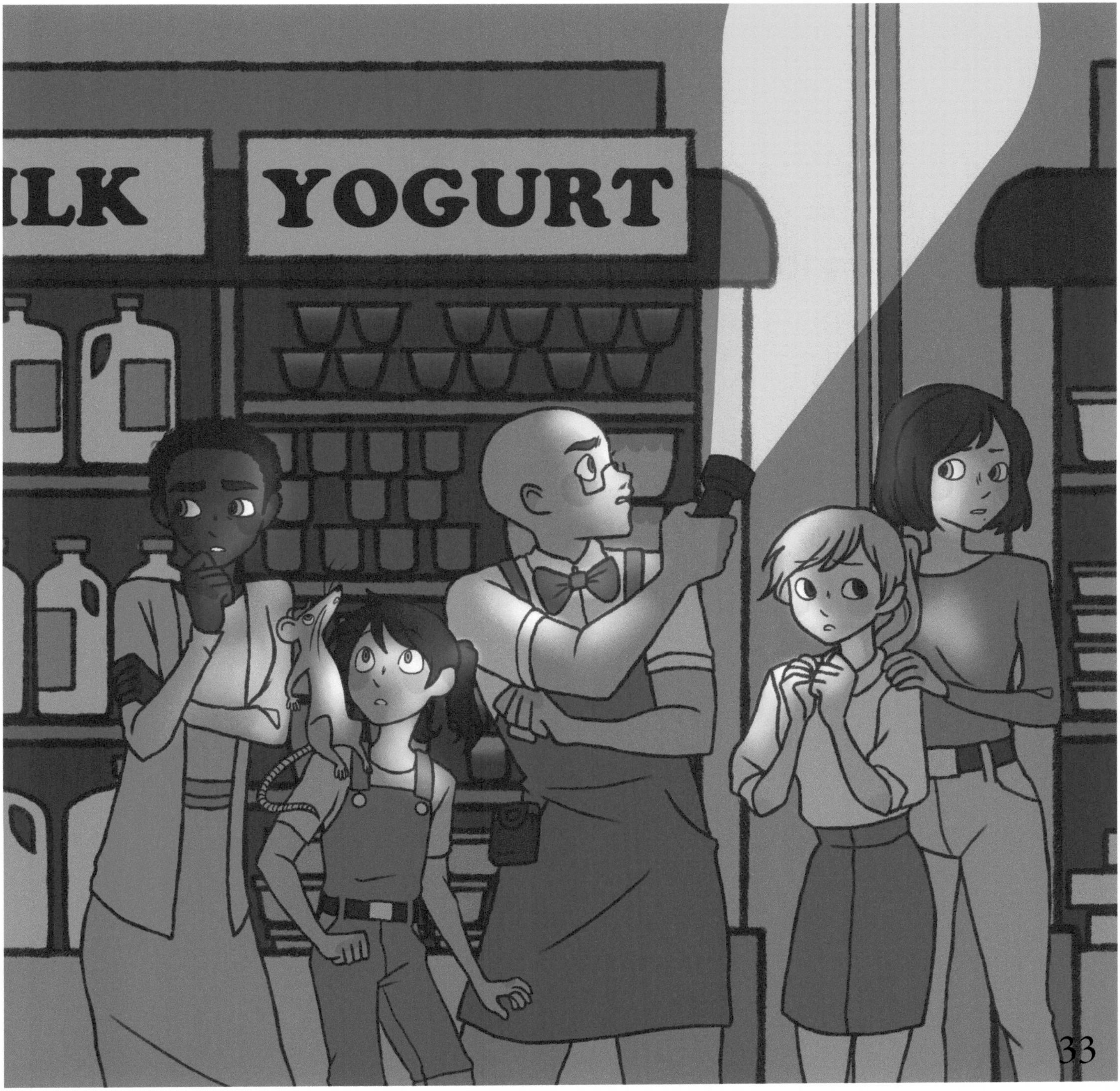
ILK
YOGURT

The beam followed the wires
up to the ceiling.
"The problem's up there," he said.
"I just have a feeling."

The light beam focused
on a broken wire.
It was twenty feet up,
or maybe higher.

"*There's* the problem!"
The manager had spoken.
"That wire is frayed.
That wire is broken."

"But I can't reach it—
it's way too high."
And I heard panicked shoppers
starting to cry.

"I know what to do!"
I blurted real loud.
Suddenly I had the attention
of the frightened crowd.

Tearing off a piece
of Dad's electrical tape,
I stuck it on Orville's back,
like a trailing black cape.

"Now climb that wall, Orville,
and do not fear.
Cling to those wires—
you'll be safe, my dear.

"But whatever you do,
don't look down.
And remember you're a rat—
the smartest in town!

"Now up you go
to find that break.
And when you find it,
use this tape."

Then Orville saluted me
with a great big smile.
And he climbed that wall,
which took a while.

Halfway up, he slipped
and was about to fall.
But his tail clung to the wires
that were clamped to the wall.

At the very top,
he slipped once more,
and I thought for sure
he'd hit the floor.

Then, in the ceiling of
beams and trusses,
Orville straightened his hat—
oh, how he fusses!

Then, on horizontal wires
running through the beams,
Orville crawled on his belly,
and then I heard him scream.

Way up high,
he slipped just twice,
making room
for scary mice!

43

There were four of them—
big and mean—
causing Orville
to suddenly scream!

So I threw the roll of tape,
causing those mice to scatter.
And Orville resumed his search,
as though nothing was the matter.

Finally, Orville found the wire
where there was a small gap.
Then he taped that broken wire,
where the wire had just snapped.

45

Then the lights flickered on
and the doors slid open.
All the people cheered
and were very outspoken.

"Hooray for Orville!
What a wonderful rat!"
Then the manager, now smiling,
gave Orville a kind pat.

"You and Orville may shop here
anytime you want," he said.
Then he straightened Orville's hat,
which underneath was still red.

Then, while talking to Mother
on my little cell phone,
we passed a postman
on our way back home.

And with a single bound
Orville was in his sack,
waving a letter at me
behind the postman's back.

"No mail for you today, Orville,"
I said.
Then he leaped on my shoulder
and rode home on my head.

The Author's dogs: Hannah, Hallie, and Pee-Pee Harley.
(Photos by professional dog groomer, Julie Rich jewlz_37@hotmail.com)

The Illustrator's dog: Tilly

CPSIA information can be obtained
at www.ICGtesting.com
Printed in the USA
LVHW070033171120
671841LV00006B/18

9 780999 785409